*A Gift from the Bride*

# A Gift from the Bride

by Gladys Yessayan Cretan

*illustrated by Rita Fava Fegiz*

*An Atlantic Monthly Press Book*

BOSTON    LITTLE, BROWN AND COMPANY    TORONTO

ATLANTIC–LITTLE, BROWN BOOKS
ARE PUBLISHED BY
LITTLE, BROWN AND COMPANY
IN ASSOCIATION WITH
THE ATLANTIC MONTHLY PRESS

Published simultaneously in Canada
by Little, Brown & Company (Canada) Limited

PRINTED IN THE UNITED STATES OF AMERICA

*For Clarence*

**M**ari watched as the bride-to-be signed the church register.

Now everyone knew that soon Mari's Uncle Vartan and the beautiful Annig would be married, and there was much happiness.

Afterward Mari stood on tiptoe and looked at the parchment paper. And she saw the letters of Annig's name written round and clear, but she could not read them.

3

"Why," she said to herself, "I may grow to be a tall lady, even a bride, and I will not know how to write my name."

Usually Mari loved to think about a wedding, and this one was to be in her own house. But now all she could think about was her wish to learn to write.

And there was no school in her village.

This was too big a problem for Mari to solve by herself. With whom could she discuss it?

Her mother and her father were busy planning the wedding and taking many trips to the village where the bride and her family lived. Everything must be done in a proper manner. In Armenia a courtship was a family affair.

Even her Uncle Vartan, who had al-

4

ways shared her secrets and helped her, had said, "Please, little *dolma,* can we talk another time? The days are short for all I must do."

In fact, Uncle Vartan had been so busy preparing his new house that he had not had even his usual time in the evenings for reading to Mari out of the book of kings and queens.

Each night Mari looked sadly at the big book, closed like a trunk full of secrets.

"All right!" she said finally. "Since they are all busy I must learn to read myself. If I try very, very hard, perhaps I will be able to read the words."

She sat next to the tall oil lamp, just as her uncle usually did, opened the big

book, and stared at the black marks on the pages. She moved her finger slowly

from one mark to the next. But the words would not come.

She sat frowning at the book and her forehead grew tighter and tighter, but the marks only stared back at her, black and mysterious.

"It is no use," she sighed. "I must go to school, and learn to read properly. But how can I do this? No girl from our village has ever traveled to the school. The boys get to go to school. Lucky boys. But not the girls. It isn't the custom."

And Mari understood the importance of custom.

The next day Mari watched everyone bustling about the kitchen, talking, laughing—her cousins and her aunts and her very busy mother.

Mari sat at a small table wrapping clusters of candy into colorful bits of silk, tying them with bright ribbons. The bride must have one to give to each guest. A big job, because it was to be a big wedding.

Everyone had been busy for weeks, sewing, baking. And now they were rolling the last grapeleaf *sarmas* for the feast, for the wedding was tomorrow.

No, Mari thought, this wasn't the time to talk about school. But it did start again next week, and if she didn't go, it might be a whole year before she could try again.

Her dark hair fell over her face, and as she impatiently pushed it back her mother looked over and laughed.

"Here, little one," she said, "let us tie the hair back with a piece of the candy ribbon. There. Now you too look like a gift."

But Mari could not smile back.

She tried to cheer herself by thinking of the bride, the lovely Annig.

How exciting to have her coming to
live right across the road from them,

10

and to be a part of their own family. It wasn't only that she was beautiful and smiled from her eyes. It was more. Annig had been to school—not only to a village school, not even only to the high school in Annig's own larger town, but to a college for girls, far away, three days' distance by wagon train.

Oh, Mari thought, the stories she would have to tell.

As she put still another cluster of candy into her large basket she saw a boy run past the window. It was her Cousin Zaven. Quickly she put down her ribbons and ran outside.

"Zaven!" she called. "Zaven!"

Her cousin turned back towards the house. When he saw Mari he picked up a pebble and flicked it right to her feet.

"Perfect!" he grinned. "What do you want?"

"Well," Mari said. Then she noticed his hair. "You look funny," she giggled.

12

Zaven pulled himself up tall.

"For the wedding," he said, "I had my hair cut by Ardash the barber." He rubbed his head. "I guess he did cut off too much. It is the first time I have been to a real barber. Besides the wedding it was because next week I start to school."

"That's why I called you," Mari said, "to talk about the school. I wish to learn to write my name, and to read stories, but . . ."

"Ha!" he interrupted, "do you think that is all we do at the school? What

about arithmetic, and what about geography?"

"What is geography?" Mari asked hesitantly.

"Why, we learn of countries far across the great oceans. Some of them even have mountains of fire," he explained proudly.

Mari shook her head in wonder.

"How I would like to learn of far-away countries," she said. "And arithmetic, too. Now please listen, Zaven. My father will not send me to the next town alone. And I wonder if I can't walk with you?"

"*Dolya!*" he exclaimed. "Have you

swallowed a toad? You know you cannot walk with the boys. How can you ask?"

"I thought perhaps, since you are my cousin . . ."

"What are you? A stranger here in our own village? The other boys aren't your cousins. It won't be allowed."

"Well," Mari answered, "perhaps I could follow a short distance behind."

"That's silly," he said. "Look, I can't stay longer. I have to go to the church and see Father Kourken about the wedding. I'm to be an altar boy. Anyway," he called as he ran off, "it's too long a walk for a girl."

"It is not!" Mari answered. She picked up a pebble and aimed it.

"Perfect!" she called as it hit his ankle. "And if I didn't have to tie bride's candies I would race you down to the church. And I would be first!"

"Mari!" her mother called from the kitchen door. "Is this a day to toss rocks like a boy? Are your candies wrapped?"

"Mama," Mari said, "I know you are busy, but please, I must talk to you

about school. Because it starts next week."

"School?" her mother asked. "What about school?"

"Oh, Mama," Mari said, "why can't I go with Zaven to the school?"

"Go to the school? In the next town?" her mother gasped. "What an idea! No girl goes alone to another town. Even if it were proper it wouldn't be safe! Have you grown up in a dream? Have you not heard of the thieves and barbarians all about us?"

She shook her head impatiently at Mari.

"Even today," she said, "I am worrying about your father returning alone when it is known that often he trades his wool for gold. And yet your father rides a swift horse for safety. You would go on foot? Alone? *Asvadzim!* Even the boys go in a group! You are not thinking clearly."

"But Mama," Mari said, "there are so many things to learn."

Her mother looked at Mari silently for a moment.

"I know," she said, "it is good to learn. If only there were classes right in our village. A few days ago our new bride was asking me why this could not be. But come, speaking of our new bride, today has its own tasks. We must prepare for the wedding."

"But the school starts next week," Mari said as she followed her mother

18

into the house, "and no one will talk to me about it."

"What is there to say?" her mother answered. "What would your father think of such ideas? His daughter walking alone to the next town. There will be fish in the treetops when he allows such a thing!"

Sadly Mari put a cluster of candy into each of the last few pink silk squares.

Her mother pulled a copper baking tray from the large stone oven in the kitchen wall.

"Here, little one," she said. "Since you are through with the candy you can take some of these poppy-seed *cheoregs* down to Father Kourken while they are still warm. They are his favorites."

The yeasty little rolls smelled so good that Mari took one for herself as she started down the winding hill with the basket on her arm.

She heard a tapping as she hurried along, and she turned to see Bedros the cobbler leaning out of his window.

"*Parev*, little Mari!" he called. "Look! New shoes! Many new shoes to dance at the wedding of your uncle!"

Mari laughed and called back, "Yes, and I have a new dress. Of course," she added importantly, "I needed it because I am part of the procession. I will toss the flower petals on the path of the bride."

Bedros the cobbler nodded. "It will be a grand wedding," he said. "The largest this village has seen."

Bedros is right, Mari thought, as she continued down the road. It will be a beautiful wedding. And my new dress is silk the color of apricots. But all I can think of is school. If I do not soon find

a way to get there I will be left home.

She turned the last curve in the road, and there, on the flat part of the town, nestled between two rocky hills, was the gray stone church, and beyond it the large well where people from both hill-sides came each day for water.

The large carved doors of the church opened and Mari saw Father Kourken step out.

"Why," she said to herself, "the *Der Hayr*. How did I not think of him? He will understand."

With this thought she ran the rest of the way, and arrived at the church steps panting.

"Good afternoon, *Der Hayr*," she said, between breaths. "My mother sends you a basket of fresh *cheoregs*, and I must talk to you. It is very important."

"Ah! Important, is it?" said the priest. "Come, let us sit on this bench

24

and perhaps share some of your mother's
*cheoregs*, while you tell me what is so
important. Have you forgotten your
duties for the wedding?"

"Oh, the wedding!" Mari said. "That
is all anyone will speak of. Please, *Der
Hayr*. Won't you be the one to listen? It
is so very important that I go to school.

But no girl has ever gone from this village."

The priest nodded. "Yes," he said. "I have dreamed of the day that we could have a school right here in the village." He munched on a second *cheoreg*. "Ah! It is a dream. But I have all I can do now. Who would teach the classes?"

"I don't know," Mari answered. "So I must find a way to go to the nearest school."

She looked at the priest. "Perhaps with the boys?" she asked hopefully. "Or even a short distance behind. I wouldn't care."

The priest shook his head. "It is never easy," he said, "to be the first to do a new thing. And this is a daring

26

thought for this village. What has your father said?"

"I didn't want to ask him until I had a plan," Mari explained. "It is important that he not refuse me. For he does not allow me to ask a second time. And," she added, "he has told me there are reasons for traditions and we must not break them."

"Yes," said Father Kourken, "but consider this. Why does your father have the largest house on the hilltop of our village, and the most farmlands? Because he has tried new farm tools and machines that many have never heard of. And why does he have the largest flocks of sheep, with many shepherds? Because at great risk he goes to distant

27

markets to sell his wool. No, your father is a man of daring, a man who listens to new ideas. And even if he were not, it

would still be only proper to talk with him. I would insist upon that."

28

Mari began to smile.

"You are right," she said. "I will meet him by the well as he rides home now. He has been away for three days, but today he returns because of the wedding."

"Remember," said the priest, "I can promise you nothing except to discuss it. The three of us."

Mari smiled. "But I can tell that you are on my side. That will help."

She ran to the ledge circling the well, and sat where she could see down the road on which her father would soon come riding home. Now for the first time she felt hopeful.

She peered down the road. She waited. She talked with villagers who

came to fill their water jugs. And some-
times she drew pictures in the ground
with a stick. But mostly she waited and
waited.

The sun was getting lower. And Mari
knew that her father never rode alone
after dark.

"He can't be much later now," she
said, and she started down the road,

tapping each bush with her stick as she passed it, and hardly noticing that she was now far from the edge of the village.

It was so hot and dusty that she decided to go even further down the road and wait under a mulberry tree.

She was swinging from one of the large branches when she spied something in the distance—a cloud of dust.

"It's Hayrig!" she said, as she dropped to her feet. "Now I can talk to him!" She ran to the center of the road, waving, as her father drew nearer.

He brought his horse to a sharp halt, and asked quickly, "What are you doing here? Is something wrong at home?"

"Wrong?" she replied. "Why, no, why would something be wrong?"

"Why are you here, then?" he asked, his voice growing stern. "If there is nothing wrong, why are you so far out of the village?"

Mari looked in the direction her father was pointing, and was surprised to see how far behind she had left the church and the well.

32

"Why," she said, "I didn't realize..."

"Didn't realize?" roared her father. "Do you think our rules are for no reason? It is dangerous to set one foot out of the village! One foot! And what of obedience? Must I explain to my own daughter that her father's word is to be obeyed?"

Mari looked down. She could say nothing.

"Come," said her father at last, and with a mighty swoop he pulled Mari up to sit on the saddle in front of him.

As they galloped towards the village again she could hear her father's voice between the thuds of the horse's hoofs ... "scoundrels ... barbarians ... only a little girl ... dangerous ..."

"But Hayrig," she said over her
shoulder, as they entered the village
and he slowed his horse.

"What is it?"

"Must it always be this way?" she
asked.

Her father's voice softened.

34

"Pray that it will be different when you grow up," he said. "But in the meantime," his voice was stern again, "see that you do grow up. Safely. You are never to leave the village. And never to walk far alone. Do you understand? Never!"

"Yes, Hayrig," Mari answered. And she knew he was right. And she knew he said it because he loved her. But she felt sad inside.

"Now," her father said, as they rode along quietly, "tell me, what brought you so far to wait for me? Is there trouble with your cousin Zaven again? Or is your cat again too high up a tree?"

"Oh no, Hayrig," Mari said, thoughtfully, "I wanted to talk to you. But I

35

think now that after the wedding will be a better time. A much better time."

"Yes," he said. "Let us turn our minds to the wedding."

When Mari opened her eyes the next morning she felt divided in half. The happy half of her whooped, "It is the day of the wedding! A sunny, beautiful day. Annig is coming! The procession. And after the wedding, the celebration."

But the other side of her was sad and dark. "The school," she remembered. "Oh, the school. I have found no way. And the time is almost here."

Her mother bustled in saying, "Up, up, up, little one. Look. They are leaving to fetch the bride."

From the window she saw all the men and boys of the family leaving in a group—her father, her uncle and her cousins.

"Mama," she asked, "will Annig's family really pretend that they don't want her to leave home?"

"Oh yes," her mother answered, "they will lock all the doors and windows. And they will answer that she is not there. One of the boys will somehow have to break in."

"How strange," Mari said, "when really it is all arranged.

"Well," replied her mother, "it is important that the bride and her family not seem anxious, even to the last. It is the custom."

"Yes," said Mari, "it is the custom. But Mama, do customs never change?"

"Not overnight, little one," her mother smiled. "Not overnight."

38

A few hours later, in the candlelit church, Mari watched Vartan and Annig as they stood before Father Kourken while he chanted the long wedding rites. Each held a tall glowing candle.

How handsome and proud Uncle Vartan looks, Mari thought.

And Annig was beautiful in her white dress with the small cluster of blue beads sewn on the full skirt for good luck. There was a shimmery silver thread tassel on each side of her face, and around her neck she wore dazzling gold necklaces of chains and coins.

Her wavy brown hair seemed to glow under her filmy veil, but she looked demurely downward, as was considered becoming for a bride.

Mari sighed with pleasure as she watched her.

And Mama, Mari thought. How pretty she looks in her blue silk dress with the bright blue velvet jacket. On her head her mother wore a small round hat from which gold coins dangled onto her forehead.

Now the bride and groom put aside their candles and turned towards each other. Their heads touched as the priest tied them together with a golden thread

42

while he chanted the ancient songs and prayers. And all the time the best man held a gold cross over their heads.

Even Cousin Zaven looked special in his white robe as he stood with the altar boys, each with his candle.

It was beautiful. But it was long, and Mari breathed a sigh of relief when they all followed the bride and groom out of the church into the bright sunlight. Now the celebration!

Mari waved to Vartan and Annig as their horse-drawn wagon started out of the churchyard, then she ran back to join the colorful, noisy procession which was winding up the hill, laughing, singing.

Towards the end of the procession was another small wagon carrying the linens and silks of the bride's dowry. Mari knew that Annig had trimmed most of these with embroidery or hand-

made lace. And she would also be bring-
ing gifts made with her own hands for
all members of her new husband's
family. Today all this dowry would be
displayed in one room of her new home.

When they reached the house on the
crest of the hill, the musicians settled
themselves under one of the large trees.

First the drummer thumped lightly
with his hands on the drum, and quickly
the other instruments joined in. The

dancers swooshed in as they heard the music, and the party had started.

At one side of the house Mari's father looked over the pits where huge roasts of lamb were turning on the fire. And Mari knew that her mother was supervising her helpers in the kitchen because already large platters of foods were appearing on the tables under the mulberry trees.

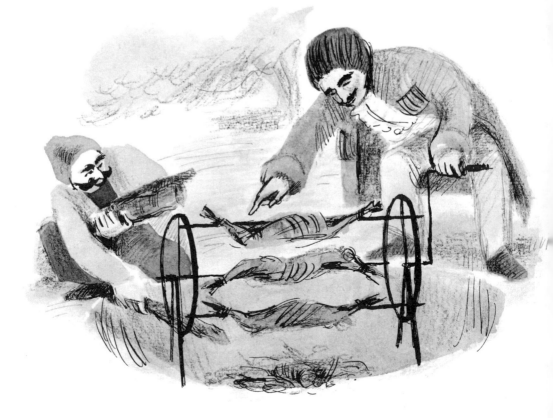

As the bride and her attendants sat
down at their special table the dancers
whirled over and danced around them
in a lively circle, while here and there
other small groups clapped in rhythm.

Mari sighed. It was all just the way a
wedding should be. Beautiful and gay.

47

But her mind kept stealing back to the thought that by now she should have found a way to go to school.

"Mari!" her mother called from the doorway. "Do you stand dreaming? Come. You may serve your new aunt her first meal with our family." She handed Mari a small tray. "And would it be possible for you to smile? Whatever is the matter with you, my pigeon? It is not a day for deep thoughts."

As Mari served her, Annig smiled her thanks. "Come," she said, "sit by me and tell me what you are thinking about."

"Well," Mari answered, "right now most of all I think about going to school. But there is no school in the village."

"Yes," Annig said. "I hope someday we may have one."

"Why, Annig!" Mari gave a small gasp of pleasure. "I know! You could teach those classes. You have been to the far college."

"How that would please me," Annig said, "but I have never studied the ways of teaching."

"But you could learn. You could surely learn."

Annig laughed. "You are so eager," she said, "that I must tell you that we spoke to your father, as head of the family, but he did not give his permission."

"His permission for what?" Mari asked.

"Why, to return to the nearest school for a year and work with the teachers. The best way of learning."

"What did Hayrig say?" Mari asked anxiously.

Annig sighed. "He thought it a good idea for the village. But he felt it would be unbecoming for me to be the only woman walking to the next village. Even in the company of my husband. I do understand," she said. "It is not the custom."

"But why should you go alone?" Mari stood up, excited. "I want to go too. And maybe Father Kourken could find us one or two more girls. Then we would be a group. And Vartan would take us all!"

"Why, Mari!" Annig said, pleased, "perhaps that will be permitted."

But Mari had stopped, her hand over her mouth.

"Oh," she said. "Oh dear. I am afraid my mother would scold me for talking to you about this on your wedding day. We should wait. But school does start next week."

"*Aman!*" Annig laughed. "Let us not start off by both being scolded. Not to-day. Let me whisper to Vartan about this soon, when he comes to sit at this table, and perhaps he can speak to your father once more. In the meantime, I have a surprise for you. A small gift. See if you can find it."

What will it be? Mari asked herself.

53

She rushed off towards the new house across the road.

As she circled the dancers she glanced back and saw her Uncle Vartan approaching the bride's table.

"Maybe she'll ask him right now," she said.

She turned into the house and saw the beautiful display of the bride's gifts. Quickly she passed the velvet slippers,

the crocheted shawl, the lace tablecloth.

Now she saw it. This was surely her gift. A small pair of mittens. But not ordinary mittens: they were of red wool,

quilted by hand, and trimmed in golden braid at the cuff. The most elegant mittens she could have imagined. She tried

them on happily, then put them back
because she wanted to be certain that
everyone saw them.

She ran out the door, smiling, then

56

she stopped. For there, standing on the steps, was her father, waiting for her.

He reached out and tousled her hair.

"So," he said, "it is a time of changes. A time of growing up. And that is why you were waiting for me yesterday?"

"Yes, Hayrig. And I hope you are not angry?"

"No," he said thoughtfully. "But tell me, why do you wish this so much?"

"Why," she said, "I must not grow into a tall lady who cannot write her name. And besides, there are many things to know. Things I wonder about."

"Yes," her father nodded. "It is the wondering and the finding out that separates us from the barbarians."

"Then, Hayrig, may I go?"

"Yes," he said, "but do not think it will be easy. It is a long walk each day. And the cold winter is ahead. Will you

sigh for the fireplace on the first bitter day?"

"Oh, Hayrig," Mari said, "you are trying to sound stern, but I can tell you are pleased. And anyway, I have some beautiful new mittens which will help me on cold days."

So it was that Mari started school. And on the afternoon of the first day she stood on the steps of the school waiting for her uncle and Annig. She was waving something in her hand.

As he walked past with the boys Zaven called over his shoulder, "Mari! What have you there?"

"I'll tell you just one thing," she said. "It isn't a toad for swallowing."

59

She held up a large paper proudly,
and there in letters round and clear was
printed

MARI

—her gift from the bride.